COL

D1493199

Books should be returned or renewed by the last
date above. Renew by phone **03000 41 31 31** or
online *www.kent.gov.uk/libs*

CUSTOMER
SERVICE
EXCELLENCE

Kent
County
Council
kent.gov.uk

Libraries Registration & Archives

C334164148

Goldilocks and the Three Bears

Boucles d'Or et les Trois Ours

Retold by Anne Walter and Fabrice Blanchfort

Illustrated by Anni Axworthy

FRANKLIN WATTS

LONDON•SYDNEY

Franklin Watts
First published in Great Britain in 2017
by The Watts Publishing Group

ISBN 978 1 4451 5834 1

Series Editor: Melanie Palmer
Series Designer: Lisa Peacock
Translator: Fabrice Blanchefort
Language Advisor: Laura Lerougetel

Printed in China

Franklin Watts
An imprint of
Hachette Children's Group
Part of The Watts Publishing Group
Carmelite House
50 Victoria Embankment
London EC4Y 0DZ

An Hachette UK Company
www.hachette.co.uk

www.franklinwatts.co.uk

Once upon a time, a little girl called Goldilocks
went for a walk in the woods.

Il était une fois, une petite fille que l'on appelait
Boucles d'Or faisait une balade dans la forêt.

Three bears were also out in the woods. Their porridge was too hot, so they had decided to go for a walk while it cooled down.

Il y avait également trois ours dans les bois. Comme leur soupe était trop chaude, ils avaient décidé de se promener en attendant qu'elle refroidisse.

Goldilocks found the bears' house in a part of the woods that she had never seen before.

Boucles d'Or découvrit la maison des ours dans une partie de la forêt qu'elle n'avait encore jamais vu.

By now, she was very hungry and she could smell
something delicious coming from inside the house.

Elle avait maintenant très faim et sentit une délicieuse
odeur s'échapper de la maison.

Goldilocks walked in and saw the three bowls of porridge.
First, she tried the porridge in the biggest bowl.
"Ouch! Too hot!" she cried.

Boucles d'Or entra dans la maison et y vit trois bols
de soupe. D'abord, elle goûta la soupe dans le plus
grand bol.
《Aïe ! C'est trop chaud !》 s'écria-t-elle.

Next, Goldilocks tried the porridge in the
medium-sized bowl.
"Yuck! Too cold!" she said.

Puis, elle goûta la soupe dans le bol
de taille moyenne.
≪Beurk ! C'est
trop froid !≫
dit-elle.

10

Then she tried the porridge in the smallest bowl.
"Just right!" she said, eating it all up.

Enfin, elle goûta la soupe dans le plus petit bol.
≪Juste comme il faut!≫ dit-elle, en finissant
de manger toute la soupe.

After breakfast, Goldilocks wanted a rest.

Après son petit-déjeuner, Boucles d'Or
voulut se reposer.

She sat in the biggest chair.
"Ouch! Too hard!" she cried.

Elle s'assit sur la plus grande chaise.
《Aïe aïe aïe, trop dur !》 s'écria-t-elle.

Next, she sat in the medium-sized chair.
"Yuck! Too soft!" she cried.

Puis elle s'assit sur la chaise de taille moyenne.
≪Beurk ! C'est trop mou !≫ dit-elle.

Then she tried the smallest chair.
"Just right!" she said. But as she was getting comfortable ...

Enfin elle essaya la plus petite chaise.
≪Juste comme il faut ! ≫ dit-elle. Mais, alors qu'elle commençait à s'installer confortablement ...

CREAK
CRAC

CRASH! The chair broke into little pieces.

CRAC! La chaise se brisa en petits morceaux.

Goldilocks went upstairs and found three beds.

She lay down on the biggest bed.

"Ouch! Too hard!" she said.

Boucles d'Or monta à l'étage et y trouva trois lits.

Elle s'installa sur le plus grand lit.

≪Aïe ! C'est trop dur !≫ dit-elle.

Next, Goldilocks tried the medium-sized bed. It was so soft that it nearly swallowed her up!

Puis, elle essaya le lit de taille moyenne. Il était tellement mou qu'il l'avala presque !

Then she tried the smallest bed. It felt just right
and she fell fast asleep.

Enfin, elle essaya le plus petit lit. Elle s'y sentit
si bien qu'elle s'endormit.

Meanwhile, the three bears were finishing their walk.
"Shall we see if our porridge has cooled down?"
asked Mummy Bear.

Pendant ce temps, les trois ours revenaient de leur
promenade.
≪Allons voir si notre soupe a bien refroidi ?≫ proposa
Maman Ours.

"Yes," Baby Bear replied, "I'm hungry!"
So the three bears hurried back for their breakfast.

≪Oh oui !≫ répondit Bébé Ours. ≪J'ai faim !≫
Les trois ours se hâtèrent de rentrer pour retrouver
leur petit-déjeuner.

"Who's been eating my porridge?" roared Daddy Bear.
"Who's been eating my porridge?" asked Mummy Bear.

≪Qui a mangé ma soupe ?≫ rugit Papa Ours.
≪Qui a mangé ma soupe ?≫ demanda Maman Ours.

"Who's been eating my porridge?" cried Baby Bear.
"They've eaten it all up!"

≪Qui a mangé ma soupe ?≫ sanglota Bébé Ours.
≪Ils ont tout mangé !≫

23

"Who's been sitting in my chair?" roared Daddy Bear.
"Who's been sitting in my chair?" asked Mummy Bear.

≪Qui s'est assis sur ma chaise ?≫ rugit Papa Ours.
≪Qui s'est assis sur ma chaise ?≫ demanda
Maman Ours.

24

"Who's been sitting in my chair? They've broken it!"
cried Baby Bear.

≪Qui s'est assis sur ma chaise ?≫ sanglota Bébé Ours.
≪Ils l'ont cassé !≫

"Who's been sleeping in my bed?" roared Daddy Bear.
"Who's been sleeping in my bed?" asked Mummy Bear.

≪Qui s'est couché dans mon lit ?≫ rugit Papa Ours.
≪Qui s'est couché dans mon lit ?≫ demanda
Maman Ours.

"Look! Someone's still sleeping in my bed!" whispered Baby Bear. "YES!" roared Daddy Bear, loudly.

«Venez voir ! Quelqu'un dort encore dans mon lit !» chuchota Bébé Ours.
«OUI !» rugit Papa Ours de sa grosse voix.

Goldilocks woke up immediately. She jumped out of the window and ran home as fast as she could.

Boucles d'Or se réveilla d'un coup. Elle bondit par la fenêtre et s'enfuit aussi vite qu'elle le put.

"What a rude little girl!' said Daddy Bear.

≪Quelle petite fille mal élevée !≫ dit Papa Ours.

Puzzle 1 / Activité 1

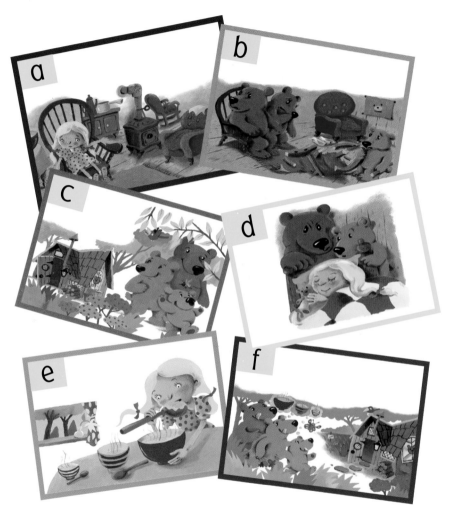

Put these pictures in the correct order. Which event do you think is most important? Now try writing the story in your own words!

Remets images dans le bon ordre. D'après toi quel événement est le plus important? Essaye maintenant de réécrire l'histoire à ta façon.

Puzzle 2 / Activité 2

1. I can run quickly!

Je cours très vite!

2. Where is the porridge?

Où est la soupe?

3. My chair is broken!

Ma chaise est cassée!

4. I'm feeling very sleepy.

J'ai vraiment sommeil.

Choose the correct speech bubbles for each character. Can you think of any others? Turn over for the answers.

A quels personnages correspondent ces bulles? Peut-tu en imaginer d'autres? Les réponses se trouvent sur la page suivante.

Answers / Repondres

Puzzle 1 / Activité 1

1c 2e, 3a, 4f, 5b, 6d

Puzzle 2 / Activité 2

Goldilocks / Boucles d'Or: 1, 4

The three bears / Les trois ours: 2, 3

Look out for more Dual Language Readers:

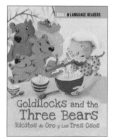

978 14451 5834 1

978 14451 5765 8

978 14451 5830 3

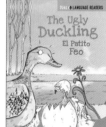

978 14451 5826 6

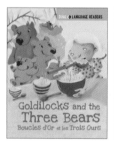

978 14451 5836 5

978 14451 5824 2

978 14451 5832 7

978 14451 5828 0

For more books go to:
www.franklinwatts.co.uk